Opposites

Library of Congress Number: 79-20525

2 3 4 5 6 7 8 9 88 87 86 85 84

Printed in the United States of America.

Library of Congress Cataloging in Publication Data

Allington, Richard L
  Opposites.

  (Beginning to learn about)
  SUMMARY: Introduces 14 pairs of opposites,
such as big and little, same and different, along
with the concept that the same object can be its
own opposite, depending upon perspective.
  1. English language — Synonyms and antonyms —
Juvenile literature. [1. English language —
Synonyms and antonyms] I. Conner, Eulala.
II. Title. III. Series.
PE1591.A52   428'.1   79-20525
ISBN 0-8172-1279-5 lib. bdg.

Richard L. Allington is Associate Professor, Department of Reading,
State University of New York at Albany

BEGINNING TO LEARN ABOUT

OPPOSITES

BY RICHARD L. ALLINGTON, PH.D. · ILLUSTRATED BY EULALA CONNER

Raintree Childrens Books · Milwaukee · Toronto · Melbourne · London

Big and **little** are opposites.
Next to the parrots, the monkey is big.

Next to the ape,
the monkey is little.

Same and **different** are opposites.
From the back, the dolls' dresses are the same.

But from the front, the dresses are different.

Old and **young** are opposites.
Next to its brothers and sisters,
the wolf is old.

Next to its mother and father,
the wolf is young.

Top and **bottom** are opposites.
The goats look as though they are at the
top of the mountain.

But they are really at the bottom.

Strong and **weak** are opposites.
This man is strong.

This man is weak.

Many and **few** are opposites.
There are many ladybugs.

Under the glass are few ladybugs.

Front and **back** are opposites.
This is the front of the TV.

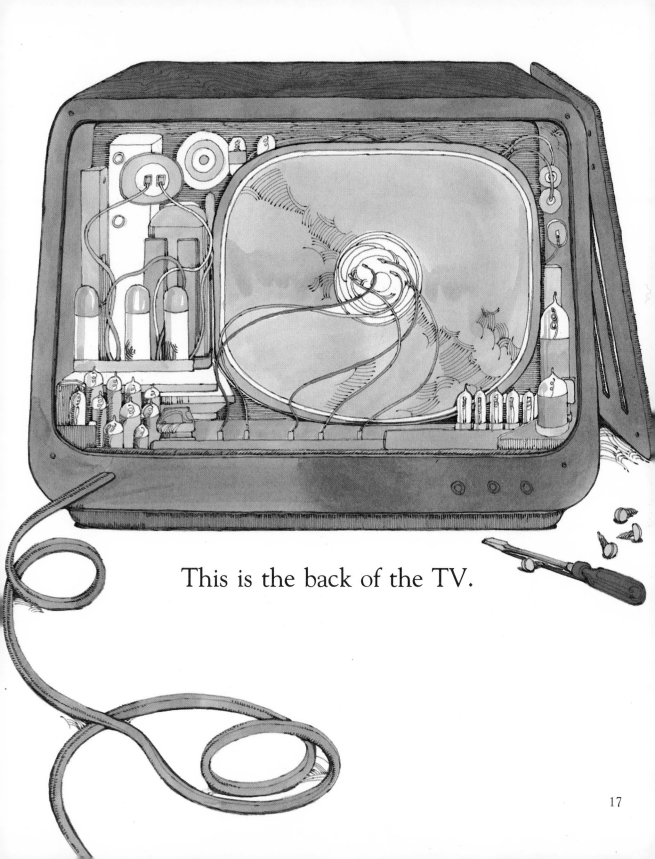

This is the back of the TV.

Tall and **short** are opposites.
Next to the house, the building is tall.

Next to the skyscraper, the building is short.

Alive and **dead** are opposites.
The flowers are alive in summer.

By winter the flowers are dead.

Left and **right** are opposites.
This is the left side of the book.

This is the right side of the book.

22

This is the right side of the book.

This is the left side of the book.

High and **low** are opposites.
At noon the sun is high in the sky.

By sunset the sun is low in the sky.

Before and **after** are opposites.
The black car comes before the red car.

The black car comes after the yellow car.

Far and **near** are opposites.
The boat is far from land.

The boat is near to land.

Over and **under** are opposites.
The bridge is over the fish.

The bridge is under the bird.

With your finger, draw a line from each word to its opposite.

tall	dead
left	low
big	back
front	short
high	young
same	weak
alive	bottom
many	after
strong	few
before	little
old	under
top	near
far	right
over	different

Make your own opposites book. Look at a newspaper or magazine. Try to find a picture for each of the words in the left column above. Cut out the pictures. Tape or paste them onto pieces of paper. Then find another picture or draw your own picture for each of the words in the right column above. Put the papers together in order and fasten them. You may ask an adult to help you.